The Boot Chronicle

A Pirateer® Adventure

Scott Peterson

James Maxwell   Chris Calder

John Gilmore

Mendocino Game Company

Cover Illustration by James Maxwell

Special thanks to:
Tom Burnap, Tom Burnham,
Courtney Dahl, Krishna Dukes,
Brian McCormick, Lennard Peterson,
Jim Rote, Sally Stewart
and Marilyn Wagner

Mendocino Game Company, Inc.
P.O. Box 1339 Fort Bragg, CA 95437

www.pirateer.com

Made with recycled paper

"Gold is most excellent; gold constitutes treasure; and he who has it does all he wants in the world, and can even lift up souls to heaven."

— Christopher Columbus

Chapter I

𝕻𝖎𝖈𝖐𝖑𝖊𝖉 𝕹𝖊𝖉

I, Ned Blast, write these lines as swords split the mossy planks over my head.

How did I, the quietest and craftiest of my shipmates, fall into this sea dog's trap? Creeping aboard this Spanish sloop last night to spy out her cargo — gunpowder, opium and silver from the mines of Potosi (and a prize greater than any of these fools can know). In the middle of a bit of lockpicking, a mere mouse of a girl poked her nose through the hatch.

"Thief!" she squeaked. "Spy!" and I was found out.

With boots pounding behind me, I ran, I crawled, I squeezed like an old rat through the ship's rotten ribs until I came here. Uggh! Warm and wet and dark it is, with a smell like the underside of a galley, as it may be.

If I'm to die in this dank place, first I'll tell of these warm seas, and the four kingdoms that rule them. Battles I have seen, and buccaneering heroes, and treachery. Now that I face my end, the stories burn inside me for telling. You who read this alone will know the world of Pirateer.

This world of water is ruled at the helm of a ship by brave captains recognizing no laws but their own. No king, queen or priest! Yet these renegades, and I am one, are treated like ambassadors by the royalty of far kingdoms, and peers by holy men and generals alike. That is, when we have those grandees in our clutches, squeezing them for the last gold flake in their pockets. Otherwise, they call us savages, "enemies of the human race."

We curse our wickedness while we stuff the hold with their loot.

Some may wonder why the seas of Pirateer aren't found on an ordinary map. Ah ha! It's no ordinary place! There are spots in the world as defy all tries at pinning them down with ink and parchment — Shangri-La, Brigadoon, the Bermuda Triangle, Mendocino. These are places of the imagination, too real for civilization's tame streets and waterways. Indeed, the way to the seas of Pirateer, and the ways of pirateering, lies on the wind of your imagination.

The path of the pirate is an ancient one. I've seen among a captain's treasure a vase, painted up by the Greeks before Rome and religion came into the world, a picture of smiling Hellenic sailors keel-hauling a set of barbarian buccaneers. And none of them with a stitch on!

My own introduction to piracy came a little more refined.

I was a lad, traveling with my parents to the Caribbean, where my father had gained a post with a trading company at Port Royal. From the moment I was carried from the dock onto that big, creaking ship, I fell in love with the sea. I remember burying my face in a rope as big around as my arm to keep from staring down into the toss of the waves below me. The smell of that rope — like all the harbors in the world — stays with me still.

We sailed under a fair star. It was August, and the summer tradewinds carried us down along the Flemish coast, through the channel that divides Dover and Normandy, south along the coast of Spain past Gibraltar. What ships swarmed those straits! Flags from every nation paid tribute at the foot of that great rock, the southern reach of Christendom.

After a couple of days, we drew within sight of the Barbary Coast, and here I noticed a change. Instead of standing on deck to watch the dolphins play, or the sea birds dive, now we sat in our cabin. My mother sewed while my father went over his papers and his pistols in preparation for our journey into the dangerous waters of the Caribbean. The captain came in several times and talked quietly with my father. He, in turn, would whisper to my mother, who would return to her needle with severe concentration.

Finally, I learned of the danger. We were being shadowed by a mysterious ship. It had appeared on the horizon off our stern three days earlier, and stayed there, like a ghost.

When the sun rose the next morning, a low, weather-black-ened sloop was much nearer, less than a league behind us. So many crawled its decks and masts, it was impossible to tell if the vessel were made of wood. Soon the terrible, gleeful shouts of the crew reached us, as the pirate ship *Magnolia* drew up for battle.

What happened next, I cannot say. I was stuffed into a

4

rough hemp sack with the cords pulled firm, then thrown into a heap of potatoes. My teeth chattered at the guns' roar and the first screams of battle. Heavy boots sounded from every direction. What seemed another lifetime was but an hour. An awful din drowned out everything, even the sea. When it eased, I knew that my worst fears had come true. Rough voices came nearer. I knew buccaneers stood just beside me. It was more than a frightened boy could take. I passed out.

When I awoke, I was lying in shade. The glare of tropical sunshine was all around me. My eyes fixed on the sky through the fronds of a palm branch. For a moment I was able to hope that all was well. Then memories and my present trouble crashed down. The wooden bars of a rough-hewn cage with branches covering the top surrounded me. The floor was made of cut planks, hoisted two sailors' height above a ship's deck. Below me and all around was the ugliest, the most outlandish, the most interesting group of faces I had ever seen.

It was a crew culled from every seaport in the world: Brits with crazily cut Navy hats trailing as many feathers as an Indian from America; Spaniards wrapped in tunics of white gauze, sword-tips nearly brushing the ground; men of the Orient, heads shaved except for thick braids down the back, gold at their belt, chest and forehead; African sailors, fierce and dignified, tall enough to reach my cage where it hung. But most of the crew was made up of Barbaries, each dressed like a sultan in silk, brilliant and royal, with jeweled sword and jeweled turban. Each stood a little apart, ruler of a separate dominion.

One of these stepped toward me, and in the same motion brought the blade of a long sword within a foot of my cage. I didn't move. Looking down, I saw a face covered with a veil. Even so, when a woman's voice, low and calm, spoke my name it startled me .

"If I cut you down, Ned, will you run?" she asked, as if asking my plans for the afternoon.

"No." The word flew between my lips without my noticing.

In a whirl of purple robes and rubies, the Barbary duchess turned to face the crew.

"He is mine!" she said. "I have found him and now I will keep him for a slave!"

A low rumble rose from the mob, but nothing more. My rescuer turned again and in one whistling arc her sword cut the rope tying my cage to the mast. I clenched my eyes shut and rolled into a ball, waiting to be slammed to the deck. I opened my eyes again. My cage rested on gently rolling timbers. She opened the latch with the tip of her silver blade.

The thick of pirates — I could smell them now, and hear their welter of languages — parted before us as Mir Al-K'haid marched me in front of her and down into the hold of the ship.

or many nights I lay in Al-Kh'aid's cabin. I missed my parents in the most awful way, asking over and over what had become of them. Al-Kh'aid would say only, "They have paid the sea's tribute."

Before long, Al-Kh'aid began sending me out to work as one of the crew. I scrubbed every beam, plank and hunk of iron or copper I could reach. Then I was graduated to slop-carrier. Finally I fought the captain's boy for a task I enjoyed — splicing rope, tying knots — and won. I'd started learning from the bottom up how to live on a pirate ship.

I sailed with Al-Kh'aid for nine years, and in that time I

mostly forgot my beginnings and learned to call myself Pirateer. Pirate I was none, and never met a self-respecting sailor who would take that tarnished name. "Pirate" is a hanging word, rounded up in the same cell as "thief" or "murderer." And "privateer" is nothing but a sea-going bounty hunter, hired to the highest bidder.

A Pirateer's in the pay of no one. We chose a life of freedom, and a name that fit. Pirateers we were, one and all.

One day on the Caribbean, with a storm after us like an angry bear, the low wolfish shape of a Madagascan xebec appeared upwind. Caught unaware, we were too late for any escape. Waves crashed across our deck as the little ship tangled us with its boarding lines and its denizens poured onto our deck.

> **"Channel stealth... way to wealth."**
>
> *THE PIRATE CAPTAIN can position her ships anywhere she chooses, but if action is her intention, then Banker's Channel is the place. Whether sailing for plunder or marauding hapless enemies, these passages are unrivaled for speed and mobility. Although dangerous, and occasionally crowded, Pirateering fortunes most oft are made here along the perilous reefs of Skull Island.*

Al-K'haid led the counterattack, and as she grabbed the ratlines to swing across, she kicked me from the mast and down twenty feet onto a stack of baled cotton. Running to the rail, I saw her land upon the enemy's deck and disappear in a confusion of swords.

We escaped that day in long boats so old that moss had grown through the oar-hafts. Our last glimpse of the *Magnolia* came as the Madagascans set her on fire celebrating their triumph. My mates considered me no good to a party faced with survival in unknown waters. This became clear on the third day, when we spied a most unusual island. Though it was small, no more than a mile across, its peak rose high above the ocean. The shape of that peak made me shiver: like a blind skull staring at the sky. My crewmates remarked on this too, but it made no difference. With winks among them, they tipped me by the ankles into the warm azure sea. After me they tossed a package that held a knife, some hardtack and a compass. I was alone.

I was on a deserted island, marooned. I knocked around the beach for weeks, keeping myself alive on what trees and tidepools could provide. And little by little I explored my island, looking for a safe place. Finally I discovered a bluff that overlooked a jungle clearing. A fresh spring bubbled in the middle of the ferny glade. And far below I could see the bay, changing shades of blues and greens by the hour. There I lived like Crusoe through the balmy winter. When storms blew in from the east, I retreated into a cave in the slope behind my hut. When sun returned, I rebuilt my little camp with what branches and timbers the winds dropped onto the jungle floor.

I was satisfied in every particular except one. I had no shoes. On deck, bare feet are no hardship. But the forest paths I now walked were another matter. I made slippers out of dried banana leaves. They split. Peeling bark from a dozen kinds of trees, I wrapped my bruised and blistered feet.

To keep from being too bored and lonely, I collected parrots. The island swarmed with them, each one a different mix of red, orange, violet, emerald. One day, on my way home from one of their favorite groves, I happened on a cave. It was bigger than most of the others that dotted this island, but curiously hidden. A sparkling waterfall, which I had walked by and drank from many times, veiled its entrance. I would have missed it again, except it was late in the day and the sun's beams fell at such an angle that the water was clear as glass, and revealed a catacomb underneath. I decided to come back when there was more light and explore this mysterious spot.

The next morning I left before dawn. On my way up the hill I noticed that the first rays of the sun fell directly on the shower of that waterfall and a broad rainbow arced across the mouth of the cave. I entered its green, dripping interior, netted with vines and sweet-smelling blossoms. Among this tropical wildness I was surprised to find a path deeply grooved into the rock floor. I lit a small torch when daylight gave way. Narrow pits were cut into the wall. In a few, dead torches still hung. I proceeded until the hallway opened out into a chamber. Before my eyes were a chest, a chair, and in the midst, in great disarray, a skeleton. A chain that ran from the chest to one bony leg told the story of the unfortunate sailor's end. One thing about this skeletal seaman transfixed me, though, and I stared frozen for a moment before I lunged.

Boots! He had heavy, thick-soled, leather knee-high boots on his bony feet. I knelt down and took my prize.

Chapter II

A Pair of Boots

f all the things I love about sailing, the smells of it cheer this old heart most of all. The whole world's in the scent of a ship — especially one that's riding low in the water with the treasures of seven kingdoms in her hold.

Cracking open a hold full of Spanish madeira or Jamaican rum, the perfume will drive a pirate crew mad. Spices and incense from the Indies — cinnamon, myrrh by the heap, essence of jasmine, jars tall as a man filled with oils meant for a queen's bed table. Honduran tobacco, Danish cheeses — a hold full of Argentine cattle smells like the sweetest treasure to a galleon full of hungry buccaneers.

And gold — those who aren't experienced think it's strange when a mate says he can smell gold. Not everybody can, of course, at least not right away. It's something that grows on you, a devilish tickling in the nostrils when you're near the stuff. Blessed as I am with this noble hook in the middle of my face, my talent is a little more refined than most. Come within a league of a vessel, I can tell you by how the fine hairs of my nose are behaving whether she's full of ducatoons or darjeeling tea.

You could say I'm right allergic to the stuff.

ut how you get treasure, and keep it — Ay, that's the trick! You need to know how to look, but looking's not enough. You need to know how to slip in and slip out, quick and quiet, but sneaking's not enough either. You need to know how to fight, how to dodge, how to wait, how to pounce.

The seas of Pirateer are beautiful — and dangerous. The shallows are a rare light blue that girls and boys know as the stuff of dreams. The deeps are brooding azure, and they've lured many an addled swabbie to join the grateful dead. They see cities down there, or treasure, or their first love — nothing you can do but let them go. Tie them to the mast and they'll just howl like dogs all night long. I'll take the peace and quiet, thanks, and good riddance.

At the heart of the seas of Pirateer sits Skull Island. For voyage on voyage, season on season, year on year, it's been the goal and prize of every sea dog and pirate empress. The approaches to Skull Island are easy, the moorings safe, the treasure easy enough to find. It's leaving the island that's dangerous. One of the first lessons a Pirateer learns is that a ship without treasure finds easy companions and allies, but a vessel loaded with booty has not a friend in the world.

Once a chase begins, knowing the secrets of the winds and currents is really the only hope a ship of buccaneers has. It's just a matter of getting back to harbor, but sooner or later you'll need every trick the ocean can provide to survive.

So it's best if I give you a little introduction to the world of Pirateer. You'll find at its four corners the harbors of the four pirate kingdoms — the rulers of this world that sits where legend and history collide.

First, under the star and crescent moon, there's the Barbaries. Of this bloodthirsty pirate nation, it's enough to tell of Keyr-ed-din Barbarossa, grandfather of the Barbary Pirates. This sea-lord made Europe's mightiest admirals weep, or more often made their wives and children weep. Barbarossa fought with storm and lightning at his sword arm — and a lie in his heart. Charles the Emperor attacked Tunis to drive out the Turks in 1529. Barbarossa, never where he was supposed to be, slipped off to the isle of Minorca, flying the flags of his Spanish and Italian enemies all the way. His corsairs attacked the capital of that island country. After a fainthearted fight, Barbarossa's men sacked and burned the place. Six thousand people were captured and ransomed, much loot carried off, and Keyr-ed-din departed well satisfied with his adventure. So those sailing under the Barbary moon and star have Keyr-ed-din Barbarossa to thank for their bad reputation.

Now for the French, under the green and gold. It's said the French are civilized, but consider Francis L'Ollonais. Started out a slaveboy and, after three long years, stowed away one night on a ship he was loading bound for Tortuga, where all true pirates go to school. After learning well his craft of fire and sword, L'Ollonais sailed to the city of Maracaibo, and when the poor terrified citizens wouldn't give up their gold to the last ounce, he killed a dozen with his sword, saying if they didn't confess where they had hidden the rest of their wealth,

Ⓧ Ⓧ Ⓧ Ⓧ **Home Port**, where all successful Pirateers end their journeys.

Ⓜ Ⓜ Ⓜ Ⓜ **Moorings**, and it's here your fleet begins. Seasoned captains learn to sail at their first opportunity. All too often, it's their last.

Ⓖ Ⓖ Ⓖ Ⓖ **The Gooseneck**, where no wise captain likes to wait. Laden vessels caught in these narrow sea lanes can be idled here for days — or perhaps a lifetime.

Ⓑ Ⓑ Ⓑ Ⓑ **Blackguard's Row**, just the place for predators to ambush a fat prize on it's way home.

Ⓦ Ⓦ Ⓦ Ⓦ **Wrecker's Rest**, the calm lagoons tucked away from the action. When the captain of a single treasure ship is badly outnumbered, a one-way run into either of these dog holes is a wicked way to deny fortune from her hunters.

Ⓡ **Skull Reef**, where treasure-bound vessels anchor to load the loot.

Ⓗ **Hell's Gate**. Wrecks litter the bottom in these waters, here at the harbor crossroads where the fiercest battles are often fought.

Ⓣ **The Tradewinds**, the fastest way (save one) to reach the ends of the ocean. But it's best not to dally there. Ships riding the trades are easy targets.

Ⓚ **Turtle Keys**, one of this ocean's prime spots. The keys control the sea for leagues surrounding Skull Island.

Ⓒ **Banker's Channel**, the quickest path to riches. But beware, pirates who start counting their money here often end up handing it over to someone else.

Ⓟ **Prayer Passage**, leading to those most mysterious Straits...

Ⓢ **The Straits**, a passage where ships can move from world's edge to world's edge. These are the places for quick escapes and lightning bolt attacks.

The Seas of Pirateer

Captain's Map

THE SEAS OF PIRATEER *are mysterious to the newcomer.*
But the wise captain knows where to run, hide and attack.

he would do the same to all their companions. They could see by the light in his eyes that he would. That day, L'Ollonais had to be satisfied with 20,000 pieces of eight and 500 fat cows, and as with all those French buccaneers, he was hungry the next day.

Some pirates just seemed to start out life as pirates — thieves without a country, you might say, sailing from birth under their own skull and crossbones. One such, though he hailed from the land of Wales, was Captain Henry Morgan. He, too, was a boy taken to be a slave in Barbados. After he escaped, Morgan tried his hand at plunder and torture — honorable occupations in his part of the world. His first great exploit was at Puerto Bello, where he and 400 merry lads took not one but two castles, using the guns of the one to storm the other. Morgan carried off 100,000 pieces of eight. He decided to take a break in Cuba, and within a month Morgan and his men had lined the pockets of every rum seller and dockside strumpet on the island. Broke, they slipped back to the sea.

Spaniards under their crimson cross are said to have been more often the prey of pirates than pirates themselves. But by my lights the Spanish were first in New World piracy by decades. Under a flag of truce the great explorer Pizarro once captured the Incan Emperor Atahualpa. The treacherous conquistador told Atahualpa's subjects that their ruler would be

released only when they had filled his prison cell with gold and silver. After the treasure was delivered, Atahualpa was killed anyway. That's a tactic all true pirates will recognize as one of their own.

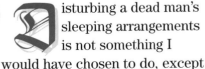

isturbing a dead man's sleeping arrangements is not something I would have chosen to do, except for those very useful boots on his totally useless feet. The boots came off easily enough — sad to say, along with one of the poor beggar's feet. But at that moment it didn't matter to me. I had my prize.

Still, before I returned to the sunlit world, I decided to take a long look around, and see if I could piece together the mystery that lay around me.

The room was empty but for the fine wooden chair, legs carved expertly, its back and seat made of tanned leather. When I approached, I noticed that its back had been engraved with a curious design. Burned into the hide was a grid — five lines vertical and five horizontal. Strange writing, unlike any language I'd ever seen, filled the squares of the grid. For a long time I looked and puzzled at these characters, but all that came clear was that I faced another mystery.

On the other side of the room was a huge chest, its peaked lid reaching over my shoulder. The latch was green with age and rust and was sealed with an ancient lock. Frustrated, I gave the chest a sharp bump with my shoulder — and scrambled sideways, regaining my balance. The chest had given way, and lay tipped on its back. It was still closed and, I now knew, empty.

I held my torch overhead and looked. Slowly the gloom gave way, and a ceiling came into view high above. As my torchlight grew steadier, I saw carved in the rock an endlessly repeating pattern of lines flowing and crossing, curving, doubling back, swirling like whirlpools, spreading into thin webs. My eyes roamed these strange patterns, until, to my surprise, the image of a face rose out of and stood complete within the bewildering design. Its eyes were furious, its jaws uplifted in a murderous howl. Another face took form at the edge of my vision, then another, a band of fierce and ancient warriors guarding either side of the passageway that led deeper into the mountain. Above that arch in clear, simple fashion was a mountain. At its heart was a star.

The cold stone floor slapped against my bare feet as I walked toward the arched doorway. The darkness pushed against the edges of my torchlight. Dank air, too long underground, breathed from the passageway as I approached, and carried to me a scent that made my nerves tickle with fear. Shaking myself, I turned, tucked my boots under my arm and started back at a trot toward the light.

I stood under the spray of the waterfall for a long time, bathed in the mid-morning sun and the sweet, rainbow-flecked torrent. I let the water fill my newfound boots again and again, and then emptied them into the stream. I pushed them under the water and ground them against rocks, determined to drive out the scent — and the luck — of their former owner.

I sat down beyond the reach of the spray and tried them on. To feel leather against my bare feet — it had been months since I'd been blessed with a real pair of shoes. I wiggled my toes. I stomped. I kicked rocks into the stream, knowing a luxury that well-shod folks can't enjoy.

Happy, I started down the mountainside toward camp. But not more than a quarter of a mile along, I felt a sharp poke in the sole of my right foot. I sat down in the middle of the trail, pulled off the boot, and shook it upside down, looking for the bit of offending gravel.

There was no gravel. Instead, a spark of green light flashed across my vision and disappeared into the brush. The hair on the back of my neck quivering, I dove after the mysterious particle. Clutching in the darkness, it was several minutes before my fingers touched something small and hard and cool.

In the center of my palm shone a cut emerald, clear as water, big enough to ransom a pleasure dome. My eyes pored over each facet of the gem, the answer to any possible wish a pirate might have. Then I laughed, thinking how worthless it was to me now.

I probed the insides of the left boot, then the right, until my fingers stumbled over a small pouch sewn into the inside leather of the right boot. Peering in, I saw the pouch, and something else as well. There was writing all around the inside of the boot. I checked the other. It too was covered on the inside with writing. Screwing up my eyes and slanting the boot leg up to the sun, I began to read. It was a list that made me gasp.

Emeralds	*6 hundredweight*
Sapphires	*2 tons*
Pearls	*16 kegs*
Diamonds	*4 buckets*
Gold Ingots	*5 crates*
Gold Braid	*325 feet*
Gold Coin	*11 chests*
Silver Plate	*26 tons*
Jade	*6 tons*

And so on ... I scanned the list that ran all around the inside:

Gold Crowns with Rubies .... *2 ea.*
Gold Throne with Gems

And at the very bottom, down in the gloom of the heel:

One Throne be thy Ruler,
One Lock be thy Key,
One's End — thy Beginning,
The Crane waits for thee.

I sat back, breathing hard, trying to realize what I had found. Perhaps my mind was overloaded with mysteries that day, for my thoughts wouldn't follow any sort of order. Distracted by my eagerness for shelter and supper, I stowed the gem in my pocket, replaced the boot and started my homeward march again. The first glimpse I had of the bay, however, scuttled any thought of contentment.

Protected by ancient coral reefs, the island's bay was calm, transparent blue. Its kelp forests, its golden sandy bottom, all were plainly visible through its crystal water. Now through the middle of the bay rode a three-masted galleon, eight-and-thirty guns by my guess, and alive with men. Boats four to a side were lowered to the water, and men dropped from the ratlines down into the boats. More desperate sailors leaped straight into the water and swam toward shore.

"Where battles flare, wise captain, beware."

A MAROONER may stumble onto any manner of watery battle-field — that doesn't mean she should jump right into the fight. Though the sight of battle makes a true pirate's blood pound, the wise captain takes her opportunity for a good look around. Choosing your spot is half the battle. Especially if the gambit's just begun, often it's best just to let the bloodthirsty wags kill each other off. After that nasty work's done, slip in and vanish with the loot!

The ships on the seas of Pirateer are of many and glorious kinds: caravels, galleons, frigates, jachts, xebecs, barcas, pinnaces — royalty of the sea.

The Egyptians believed that the ships they built were living things — they painted eyes on the hull so their craft could see along the foggy, reedy old Nile. I say they weren't far wrong. Every ship I've been on has had its character — some cowards, some heroes, some pranksters.

The caravel is a ship that made history. Henry the Navigator, Prince of Portugal, took it from being a fishing boat to the first craft that ventured along the coasts of Africa in the 13th century, while looking for a passage to India. She gained eternal fame in 1492: the *Nina* and the *Pinta* were both caravels. Shallow-drafted and swift, they were nimble among the strange new isles and shoals of the West Indies. Columbus' own ship, the *Santa Maria*, not a caravel, was something bigger, and he complained all the way across that he, the great Colon, had the slowest ship of the bunch.

The galleon is supposed to have been invented in Spain, but it popped up in so many places during the middle of the 1500's that several crowns have claimed that prize. Queen Elizabeth sent galleons against the Spanish Armada, and they served as the mightiest vessels on the sea for nearly a century. A bit fancy for my taste: mizzenmasts, topmasts, topsails, lateens, quarter-deck, halfdeck, poop deck, but they're fearsome vessels of war.

The frigate was the next bully on the scene. It started small, six or eight guns, but by the 1600s, the English had a frigate hauling four-and-sixty cannon. Bristling with weaponry and explosives, by the time the frigate took over, the joys of ramming, boarding and buccaneer bluffing had to take a backseat to raw firepower.

Small craft still had their place. Take the Dutch jacht. About half the size of an ordinary frigate, it was used mostly for communication and ferrying the powerful about. In darkness or fog, though, a jacht is just the thing for sneaking up on some wallowing cargo ship. In fact, "jacht" originally meant "swift craft" or "hunter." Unfortunately, the jacht also gave the world "yachting" when Charles II of France built a small armada of them ... so he could watch them *race*, the sluggard. Kings leave me sour! What a waste of good shipbuilders.

The barca and the xebec are also small but useful craft. Both started in the Mediterranean, where wind is often hard to come by and large vessels lie becalmed for weeks. The barca's a low, forward leaning thing, great for speed and narrow places. Same with the xebec — lean, with very little space for cargo. The Barbaries introduced xebecs to Europe, terrorizing the traders of Venice and Spain so badly that the proud merchants of those prosperous regions had to lower themselves to copying the barbarian. It's said that, when it's properly sailed, only a xebec can fight a xebec.

The pinnace of Holland seemed to be everywhere in the 1500's and 1600's. The Dutch around that time boasted of having 100,000 sailors on 10,000 ships, and most of those ships (though I don't believe they had half that many) were pinnaces. Just as good for fighting as trading. A little smaller than a regular frigate or a galleon, they often sported two foresails well out ahead of the prow, making it a matter for joking that a pinnace looked like it was always about to blow its nose.

The Spanish galleon's boats reached shore, followed not long after by their flailing crewmates. The men started across the beach, grouped in fours and fives, heading for the rocks that rimmed the sand. Soon they were hard at work, lifting and carrying large, round, heavy objects from shoulder to shoulder among them. These dark ovals they dropped into pieces of canvas spread lower down on the beach. When the canvas was filled, a squad of men folded it and dragged it to the water's edge, then into the small surf, and loaded it into a waiting boat.

I needed a closer look.

I scrambled lower onto the bluffs that stood just over the beach. From my new spying place, I could see the ovals they carried were moving. Slowly they rolled — I could see heads now, and blunt brown forepaws. *Turtles!*

These creatures by the dozen lay sleeping among the rocks. The turtles had just returned from their egg-laying cruise of a thousand leagues when they don't stop to eat for weeks at a time.

Who these scavengers were I determined to know, since they offered my one way off the island. I moved down closer until my knees had sand under them, so close I could see the streams of sweat on the backs of the sailors as they hauled their loads down to the waiting boats.

> **"Hunters stray who cross their prey."**
> *THE HUNTING CAPTAIN takes a position straight behind her prey, putting the winds in her favor.*

> *Striking in a straight line is always the surest path. The skill of the hunted lies in moving sideways away from the hunter. Making them turn a corner to attack is the ticket.*

But there was more shocking work afoot on my formerly lovely beach. Another group of sailors — like all the rest, shirtless and in torn sack-cloth trousers — was at work on some devious piece of machinery. They set up wooden stakes taller than themselves. Then, one sailor standing on the shoulders of another, they hammered the posts into the sand. Others laid out yards of the strongest hemp and laid these over the beach in criss-cross patterns. This contraption, 40 feet across, took shape next to a tall palm tree. Its thick top, tunnelled with the nests and food bins of the island's birds, sat atop a smooth trunk swaying high in the warm afternoon breeze.

A small corsair materialized from behind the larger ship

and made for the beach. It had one black sail, and burnished
iron shields lined the deck. One iron spike struck out from its
bow, beckoning war.

The ship turned just outside the breakers and lowered a row-
boat. Guards dressed — if you liked to call it that — in the
tanned hides of a dozen different animals climbed in. Last came
a barrel-shaped figure, his pear-shaped frame fit tightly in a velvet tunic. Instead of climbing down into the waiting boat, he
swaggered up and down at the rail shouting, gesturing like an
actor. His audience below looked up amazed, but their attention
didn't seem to satisfy this odd captain. For the captain, I could
only guess, he was. First his gloves, then his helmet, and finally
his boots, he hurled down on their heads. They still kept their
seats under this hard rain. When he had finished, they quietly
gathered up his things while he climbed down among them.

With a great flourish of his sword, the captain ordered his
landing boat to depart. Oars bit the water, the craft surged
through breaking surf and onto coral sand.

Here and there along the beach, turtle poachers kept up their
work in tight, frenzied swarms.

When he reached the sand, the captain stood with his legs
planted firmly and wide apart, his fists burrowed into his pliant
sides. He surveyed the beach, the strange machine, the turtle
raid, all with a long, smiling gaze. At the captain's side hung a
whip coiled round and round. His left hand rested there.

Another brace of guards followed, and as I watched the pro-
cession, it seemed to me again that I'd seen this band before.
Where and when and who floated just outside the reach of
thought. But I knew that when it returned, the memory wouldn't
be a pleasant one.

Then came a sight that answered my question and froze me
with shock at the same time. Supported by a guard at each
elbow, Mir Al-Kh'aid, dressed now in the plain white of a slave,
chains around her waist, climbed out of the boat.

They led Al-Kh'aid before her captor, and forced her to her knees. She stared at the sand. As if to show kindness, the captain laid a stubby hand on the top of her head. Then the soldiers jerked her to her feet.

Moving on at a bouncing gait, the captain headed up the beach. His voice broke angrily on the tranquil air, and the workmen jumped. Grabbing ends of the rope, they sprinted, some toward the driven stakes, others toward the nearby palm tree.

One man, reaching the tree at a dead sprint, didn't break stride as he scrambled up its trunk. Another threw a line, and the tree-climber tied it securely just below the fronds. He fastened another rope and then another to the shuddering tree. The rest pulled down on the lines, bending the tree headdown to the ground. As soon as the lines were secured to the stakes, a pair of shaven-headed slaves ran up with a net and fastened it to the treetop.

The captain and his guard gathered in a crescent scrutinizing this work. A crowd grew behind them. Even the turtle gatherers stopped what they were doing to peer down the beach. From within a tight group of guards a man was produced, held by his arms and legs, struggling. Whipping his head from side to side, crying out, he was desperate for his life.

He had good reason to fear. Arriving at the palm tree, the guards trussed their captive securely and unloaded him into the net. They drew their swords.

"If you try to escape, you will be hacked to pieces," the captain roared, enjoying himself very much.

The captain regarded his prey with a calm, contented look. But the scene before him made his mildness more terrible. Half-turning toward his crew, bellowing so I could hear him from my hiding spot, he shouted out a question:

"What weapon is a pirate never without, but never owns?" I

heard the captain roar.

There was a brief silence. The man may have answered, or just run out of time.

"His thoughts!" thundered his torturer, "His thoughts!" and staggered back roaring with laughter. Still laughing, he brought his arm up and then down again. Steel flashed in the late afternoon sun and a rushing sound like great birds cut through the air. The palm tree shot upright and a dwindling speck arced across the sky, a weary and wandering cry trailing behind. The poor soul disappeared into the jungle.

I was shaking when I looked back to the beach, where I saw another struggling unfortunate being loaded into the net. Another victim was dispatched in the same way, and another. By the last, most of the crew had turned away, as if even they were embarrassed at such a display of sadism. But they didn't seem surprised at this behavior on their captain's part.

The contraption was taken apart, ropes untied, stakes pulled, palm tree released from its ugly duty.

But soon this fun met its end, as the last of the turtles were being picked up. Frantically, I looked around for a way aboard. Down the beach a cluster of men was working at something — a turtle shell wedged into the sand. Here and there along the beach these great shells, like the old shields of giant warriors, lay beached and half buried in the sand. A squad of men hauled them out of the sand and tossed them onto a canvas. Seeing my chance I slithered on my belly through the sand until I reached the nearest hollow hulk. I blessed my scrawny frame — hard diet and hard work had kept me less than one hundred pounds — as I jammed into the dry, sand-filled chamber.

My fortune lay in how these fearful sailors hurried. Down the beach I had seen them knocking the sand from shells with brutal kicks. But now they cursed their comrades for breaking from the beach so early, leaving them with their assigned chore yet to do, and sails already struck. So these wretches simply yanked the shells free and tossed them, sand and all, onto the canvas.

"**They best defend who linger behind.**"

ONE SURE WAY to protect a treasure ship is to follow it, the way porpoises swim and sea birds fly. They're *watching each other's backs, and there never was a better pirate's defense than putting a few tons of ship between you and an enemy. When a captain takes a treasure ship home, lots of times she'll make sure to have her escort lined up ahead of time.*

When their growling voices came near, I jammed my arms and legs against the shell's strongest places. After a short ride down the beach and onto the boat, I was nearly beat unconscious while being hauled aboard — thrown together in a net with a dozen or so turtles, banged against the side of the ship every foot of the way up. Finally, I was deposited into the hold, and I welcomed the darkness.

I waited for hours, until the deck grew quiet. Seven bells sounded. I waited longer, until nothing but the ship's groans and the occasional watchman's call crossed the night. Another sound reached me. This was from below. Low mutterings and then groans, very soft, floated up from the darkness underneath me. At first I crossed my heart against spirits, knowing the hold of many a ship echoes with the cries of captive souls. But soon I realized the living, not the dead, made this strange scraping and moaning. The turtles were stirring.

I peered out of my shell. Before me was a great, soft eye. Swirls of gold and copper surrounded a drop of sea green at its center. The leathery face, so close to mine, looked at me with the mildest curiosity, and I wondered if this fellow creature knew its fate.

A glare of torchlight reminded me of my own likely end. I jerked my head back into the shell, giving it a good whack that sent a deep, hollow gong echoing through the hold.

"Strange sounds these *creatur's* make," a voice said above me, and voices grunted in answer. I lay without breathing while the sailors gaped and joked at their strange cargo well into their evening ration of grog. Suddenly, their mumbling turned to shouts and whooping laughter.

"What'er ye doin' with yer iron, squirrel?"

"Ay, keep it that way!"

"Don't be flyin' it at me!"

> "**T**reasure found — homeward bound."
>
> *THE TREASURE CURRENT: that's what baffles and beguiles so many sailors, thinking the game's won when her loot's in the hold. Once your vessel's weighed down with gold, the treasure current takes over: you'll go no direction but homeward. But only fools take the first dash that way. Many a wily captain's sat her treasure vessel in the lee of Skull Island until the way home is clear.*

A crashing explosion lit the hold. What seemed like a thousand ricochets followed, and the sound of splintering shell. The sailors were in full riot. The gunshots — one followed another — awoke the blood madness in them. Now they cheered their mate as he sent pistol balls slamming down into the hold at a furious rate. The turtles flailed in terror, beating blunt limbs against each other's stony backs.

These sailors, apparently, had watch of the deck. All their havoc raised no one. I slipped from my shell as another powder blast roared down. Scrambling over the turtlish landscape, I reached the bulkhead and crept along within its shadow. Ahead of me, a ladder's rungs stood out in the moonbeams.

My fingers were on the ladder in a moment. I reached the top, and nudged the hatch ajar. Their backs were toward me, rapt in their game.

A long boarding pike, twelve feet tall and big around as my wrist, stood upright, lashed to the mast. It was a fearsome weapon, but it weighed nearly as much as I did. Bursting from my hiding place, I ran full out across the deck. There were four of them. One in a cap with a ridiculously long and battered feather tipsily loaded his pistol.

I unlashed the pike and took it at a full run toward the sailors guffawing over their mayhem. The whistle of solid oak through thin air was all the warning they could have had. Head-high at a full run I swung the pike, and it did its work. The four pitched forward into the blackness. All that remained was the pistol that had clattered to the deck.

I picked up the weapon, looking every second for more adversaries. There were none. Slamming the hatch shut, I left the four to sleep with the turtles.

 summer night sky clear of all cloud and mist hung close over the ocean. Starlight collected among the swells, and the moon reflected everywhere in diamond clusters. A soft wind brought the sound of the surf and the smells of the island forest. Jasmine, grapefruit blossom, and honeysuckle mixed with the sea's mighty tang seized me for a moment. It was nearly my last.

I raised my happy nose and closed my eyes. A knifeblade buried itself shivering in the mast beside my head.

Instantly I dropped ready to run or fight. Still, I saw no one. The deck and rigging creaked. I looked again at the silver blade buried three inches into the wood. A faint design marked its base: the emblem of Al-Kh'aid's Barbary fleet.

I looked once more in the direction indicated by the blade. This time, in a tiny porthole amidship, I glimpsed a flash of white appear and vanish.

"The blade!" Her voice reached me. Yanking the knife free, I ran across the deck.

Her face had grown thin in her months as a prisoner, but it had lost none of its dignity, and her black eyes burned. She smiled as she took the dagger from me.

"Don Castillo is drinking in his cabin. He'll call for me soon. This blade is for him."

"You'll kill him?"

"Yes. He is fool enough to let me come near him. He mistakes me because he flatters himself with cowards and buffoons. And after I kill him, and they kill me, they will drink to me and make a song about me. Hide now, and wait. You'll know when I'm done. Then — escape!"

She turned from the porthole.

"But we can both escape!" I pleaded.

Her voice now was flat and cold. "They are too strong."

She was gone. I was desperate. But another voice interrupted my worries.

"Sail Ho!" piped a boy far up in the rigging. And though pistol fire wasn't worth a look, now from hatch and from cabin, Castillo's crew burst out.

I melted into a corner and watched as a sailor, tattooed everywhere but his eyelids it appeared, climbed the rigging and looked. He pointed across the bow and all heads turned that way. Out on the night sea, a small shadow moved against the stars. This vessel was expected, for once Castillo's crew spotted it, they beat swords on plank and cannon and put up an awful din.

A great fiery light broke out behind me, bathing the whole scene in a rippling glare. Everywhere torches were being lit, and next to Castillo burned a great cauldron of flame. The captain emerged at the head of his guard.

He set to his devilish work again, throwing the lash of his whip out across the deck, raking the backs and heads of his crew. Though they set up a howl, they kept to their work. It seemed they were readying the ship for departure once the rendezvous was done.

The black ship was approaching. I recognized it now as the one that overcame us at sea and took Al-Kh'aid captive. Torches burned aboard her now, too, and the din and chants of her crew carried across the waves.

I knew that Al-Kh'aid could not carry out her fatal plan. The crew was in a frenzy, the captain immersed in his sadistic pursuits.

Castillo stood, whip at his side, silhouetted in the glare. He took a step forward, and then stumbled, hopped sideways, and then tumbled forward, as if his feet had been pulled from under him. But when he hit the ground, one leg jerked straight up. He turned upside down. Before an amazed crew, the captain left the deck jerking rapidly upward. One leg taut, the other hung sideways while he spun crazily like game on a line. Castillo was hanging from a noose around his ankle.

The crew was dumbfounded. Al-Kh'aid stepped forward, a fearsome figure in the torchlight. She held a pistol and a cutlass high over her head and called out in a clear voice.

"Throw off the lines, weigh anchors! We save ourselves together!"

The crew hesitated. I smelled my opening. Leaping from my corner into the ratlines, I scrambled up to the nearest fighting top. It was empty, except for a cohorn, an odd, squat gun that threw its ball in a long, high arc. Hoping its range would bring the shot somewhere near the approaching ship, I struck a spark from the flint of my pistol against the cannon's base ring. The weapon flashed and roared, knocking me down. The noise threw the galleon's crew into even worse confusion. Each looked balefully at the others, their courage — or just their rage — drained by this shift in their fortunes.

"Harbor lane, enemy's bane."

DEFENDING OR ATTACKING, the best place for your vessels near its harbor is in the lanes leading to port. Ships on the open sea can take any path they choose.

But homebound ships have but one path. Who controls a harbor's approaches decides who comes and goes and who sinks.

Now the black ship, its crew made furious by the attack, sent off a first volley. It tore the sails and sent clouds of iron humming over our heads. I was already twelve feet up in the ratlines when I got hold of a line and swung over the bewildered heads of the sailors to join Al-Kh'aid. She took up Castillo's whip, which lay draped over the railing in front of her, and cracked it like thunder over the deck. The crunch and groan of the anchor chains sounded at about the same time as the first roar of our cannons.

The xebec soon had to keep her distance, badly outshot by our galleon. Before we were clear, though, she put a hole a horse could walk through just above our waterline.

When we reached the open sea, we would have to make immediately for a port where we could anchor and make repairs. The black ship was again only a shadow on the dawn horizon. Castillo swung high up in the moonlight. Behind the *Garcia*, turtles turned again to their home on the sea.

Chapter III

Planked!

rrows arcing flame into the sails, cannon-ades at close range, battering rams against a schooner's prow, captives terrorized with the most fantastic threats of torture and may-hem – the life of a Pirateer is awfully barren without a little excitement now and then.

For ten years I captained the *Garcia*, hauling in treasure the likes of which Castillo's old crew had never seen. Our success drew two more ships, and we were a fleet. But after all the good fortune I brought them, how I came to be at the end of a plank one day will tell you something about Pirateers.

y emerald was usually kept hidden on a high shelf on the bulkhead in my cabin. My boots — and their secret — were my closest companions.

Being a captain, I had other things to busy my mind. But the thought of the mysterious treasure never left. Years passed, and we were in the West Indies again, when those strange clues and memories began shaping my destiny.

One day we sat becalmed in the middle of a long, dry cruise. Restlessness came over the ship like a foul wind. By afternoon there had been three fights. I considered doubling the day's ration of grog, when a sailor burst on deck. He carried something in his fist, waving it over his head. He was Grinning Jack, named because of the grin he always carried on his face. It was no real grin, though. Jack was one of the sourest sailors I ever let aboard the *Garcia*. He'd won that grin in a fight, when a blade glanced off the side of his face and cut the muscle. Ever after, Jack sported his lopsided leer, and that's what he turned on his crewmates.

Leaping onto a powder keg he began shouting in a hoarse voice, "Gather 'round! Gather 'round! Treachery!"

The crew lay in one of those listless funks that can cover storm clouds. Few paid Jack any attention at first. I noticed that as he yelped he threw shifty glances in my direction. Then with a dramatic gesture, he held the object high. It was the emerald. Jack was a carpenter who had a bad habit of perusing the property of others in the course of his work. It was well known that my personal belongings were not to be touched. But Jack, I saw, had let his curiosity get the better of him, and possibly me.

"This I found in the captain's cabin," said the smiling one.

Now he had a crowd growing around him. A mutter ran through the entire ship.

"Say — it's a present from his *mither!*" a sailor cried. The crew, now roused from their daydreams, roared with dangerous laughter.

See, during our last shore turn on Maracaibo, the entire *Garcia* crew, myself also, ran out of money. Quite a few sailors ended up in a debtor's cell. The rest of us put together what we had and ransomed them. It was understood one of us was as broke as all the others. But this gem I had always kept aside, and it would have bought three ships' worth of bankrupt sailors.

Still, I had committed a cardinal sin of captaining: holding out on the crew. I knew the punishment.

"*Plank 'im!*" the cry went up.

In a moment, my men were passing me from hand to hand over their angry heads, tearing at my collar and buttons while landing several painfully accurate punches along the way. I found myself at the end of a slim piece of wood freshly hung over the roll of the sea. That morning, I'd started out as their captain. Now it looked like I would be their sport. I looked down: black fins sliced through the swells.

Puffing himself up, my smiling nemesis put his questions to me.

"How come you by this *jool?*" he demanded.

I didn't answer, but as I measured the situation, I could see that this bargain was not working my way. I needed something to change the situation, something their fear and greed, fueled by boredom, could gnaw on for a while.

"How came you ..." he began again in a loud voice, but I interrupted. Clearing my throat, I paused. Then I started to sing, starting out low and growling ...

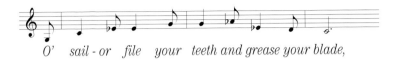

O' sail - or file your teeth and grease your blade,

They'd heard this one before — I'd used it as a pirate's lullaby.

And lis - ten to my prof - it - a - ble song,

Their eyes looked far away.

So oft are Pir - a - teer - ing for - tunes made,

Dreamy smiles began to appear on their faces.

Sail - or file your teeth and grease your blade!

By the time I was into the second verse, I had their ears, and I sang out loud and clear.

There's emeralds by the hundredweight arrayed,
And sparkling sapphires hoarded by the ton.
Pearl fountains and a waterfall of jade,
Sailor file your teeth and grease your blade.

A Mayan throne of gold with gems inlaid,
Bright ingots thick as thumbs and rubied crowns
With diamonds heaped like gravel from a spade,
Sailor file your teeth and grease your blade.

For silver plate we hunger, golden braid,
Let's drink and drown this blasted treasure lust,
With chests of ducatoons that never fade,
Sailor file your teeth and grease your blade.

Speak up, hearts, are you buccaneers or slaves?
Are shackles, lock and lash your only wage?
So oft are Pirateering fortunes made,
Pirate file your teeth and grease your blade!

The song had a marvelous effect: At first, my audience
hesitated. Then, the three who held me at swords' ends

 started to grin. They thought
I'd gone balmy with fear. But I
grinned back at them and
started into my best jig.
They'd never seen a man
twirling on one toe out at the
tip of a gangplank before.

From the first time I
uttered the words
"Pirateering fortunes," I knew I wouldn't walk the plank
that day. A blank but hungry look passed over the faces
before me. The deck quieted; men lowered swords, whips
and pistols to their sides. The catalog of treasure begun,
low murmuring began to rise up from the mob. Blades
began to keep time, tapping against wood and iron. My
dance grew wilder — I shouted the words to my song
with a furious joy that spread like sparks on a parched

thicket. Soon, I could see signs of a riot.

They threw back their heads and roared, eyes wide and glazed, as if looking at a tubful of diamonds already. Now, when I reached the lines they knew, they joined in a terrifying chorus:

Pirate file your teeth and grease your blade.

I joined the celebration, knowing I had bought time — hours or days I didn't know. My three guards had abandoned their mission and now sang with the happy faces of children. You'll often see an old buccaneer, trousers tattered at the knee, most likely with an odd number of limbs, counting off beads on a yellowing coral necklace. He's not saying a rosary. He's remembering his treasure tale, counting booty he probably never saw.

Somehow in all our havoc, someone spotted a sail.

"Mates!" I called. "We'll test our neighbor's pockets. If they're lined, we'll strip 'em! (Up went a happy cry) If they're empty, we'll leave him on his way with a few stripes on his back for disturbing our merriment. (Another cheer) To posts! To arms!"

The crew raced below me, priming cannon, clearing lines, readying everything for the fight. The stink pots were broken from their casks and hoisted high, ready to be lit and launched. We could defeat an unwary ship with their own noses and weak stomachs by torching these kegs of saltpeter, brimstone and asafetida and throwing them down upon the unfortunates' deck.

But this time it wouldn't be necessary. The flags this ship flew were like none I'd ever seen.

Drawing within sight of our telescopes, the French-flagged frigate ran up its banners. Through the glass I read: "Peace" ... "Welcome" ... the next one I struggled to make out. It was a series of flags that seemed to be spelling out ... "roast lamb."

Unsure if this last was referring to us, or perhaps some odd kind of code, I charged the crew not to let down their guard. The frigate was powerful — four and sixty guns on three decks, armor and high barriers along her sides, deck swimming with a hive of lean sea wolves. All in all, a fearful war machine.

But as she grew nearer, I began to see strange things. Not only ratlines and tackle hung from her masts, but draping streamers — gold, green, scarlet. Casks of grog and blackened haunches of smoked meat were strung up at intervals over the deck. On the poop deck appeared — I pulled my eye from the glass, rubbed both, and looked again, yes! A table, a white cloth, a platter with some grand fowl on it — *garnished.*

By the time the frigate reached hailing distance, the *Garcia's* whole company stared gape-jawed at the floating banquet. Its crew stood at the railings as well, jeering and joking and having a fine time.

One figure stepped out from the rest. At first I thought he was riding on the shoulders of the ones on deck. But when he threw a huge leg aloft and planted one tremendous boot on the deck railing, I knew we faced a giant.

Eight feet, nine feet — this man stretched skyward like no other man I'd ever seen. The grand curve of his shaved head seemed to be muscled itself. One heavy gold hoop hung from his ear. His left hand played over the hilt of his sword.

"Hail merry thieves!" he called. "We've come from bloody work. Three Spanish galleons we met at the straits. The fight was glorious, a well-spent day, for certain. But two of our ships and two of theirs are at the bottom of the sea. Perhaps you've never seen French gentlemen mourn their comrades. We have plans, *mon* buccaneers, for a feast, and something better than a feast. But we need to swell our numbers as well as our bellies. Join us! Bring swords and sidearms, however you feel safe. But join us!"

At that, canvases were yanked from three long tables that

ran the length of the main deck. They were arrayed with all the riches of a tropical banquet. So strange was the scene, so alluring the spread, the crew of the *Garcia* wasted no time.

Before we had reached his deck, Leon started the tale of his fight with the Spaniards, a scene that played itself out hundreds of times on these warm waters. And of course, being captain, he made sure his own heroism was clear.

There are pirates, and there are those who are something more than a pirate — a pirate captain. Those who captain ships on the seas of Pirateer must command the awe of pirates, and that's no easy task. Some try to do it with bluster, but not for long. Some try pure meanness — captaining a ship by their very teeth. But teeth come out too easily.

The great captains have all done it one way — with their brains. Brave, sure, fierce, crafty: the pirate captain is all that. But she also — always — knows just one more thing than everybody else around her.

Captains come in many kinds, but by and large you'll find them to be three kinds: the greedy, the malicious, and the treacherous.

Among the malicious was Roc.

Roc? What kind of a name is Roc? A good enough name when you've lost any other. Somewhere along the way Roc let go the name he was given, so he took up the first one he found. His piratical bent showed early. As soon as he'd grown taller than a table leg, Roc aimed at bloody buccaneering and ran off with a likely band when he was only eleven. Only six years passed before his mates offered him a command. On his first voyage Roc seized a Spanish sloop loaded with silver bullion and sailed to Jamaica, a great haven for English buccaneers. He amazed all with his rages and his wiles, and soon Roc became known as Head Pirate of the West Indies. Every buccaneer vied to sail with him. Only the best got a chance.

It's often told how awful Roc was in battle. When a ship crossed his path — woe if it be a Spaniard — he attacked without fail. He preferred mayhem to gold most times. But Roc's true colors didn't show until he was ashore, where one of his favorite things to do was to drink. In this state he fancied the whole world as his playground. His method of play was to sneak up on the unsuspecting and take a whack at them with his cutlass. Sometimes he used the flat of the blade, sometimes the edge. Constables were in short supply on the streets of Havana and Kingston and the other pirate burgs, so "Head Pirate" Roc was a law unto himself.

Τhe treacherous captain is something else again. Treachery wears a finer habit than malice, and its face never had a better model than Edward Teach: Blackbeard.

Just one tale will do — Blackbeard (his beard was indeed black and voluminous, and woven into braids with colored ribbon and twine) was sitting at his captain's table with three of his officers. When they had done with a fine and heavy meal (all of Blackbeard's appetites were both complicated and extreme), the Captain unholstered two of his pistols and lay them in his lap. One companion remembered something to do on deck and took his leave. The two others sat wide-eyed, waiting to see what their leader would do. He fired, hands crossed, sending a ball into the knee of his first mate. The other shot knocked a china plate down from his cabin wall.

His men asked in amazement why he behaved this way. "I must

shoot one of my men every so often," Blackbeard answered, "So you will remember what kind of person I am."

Greedy captains are likely to be young captains, for they don't often grow old cheating their crewmates.

Henry Morgan was another of that scarce tribe that set out from boyhood to become buccaneers. He fled his Welsh farm while still in knee-pants and signed on for three years in Jamaica. When he got there, young Henry discovered he had sold himself for little better than a slave. But his three years did end, and Morgan made immediately for the pirate lairs of Jamaica. He fell in among a likely band and soon took to his bloody toil.

But Morgan had a hunger that led him to acts more desperate and despicable. Many times he lost all he had. His way in those situations was to try to steal something right away of equal worth, or rather twice the worth of what he'd lost. This he

"Straits are rare for a pirate's lair."

ONE OF THE TRUE MYSTERIES of Pirateer is the Straits. At each end of the sea is a narrow passage leading ... where? Those brave enough to try and skilled enough to succeed end up clear on the ocean's other side, quick as light. Running the Straits can be dangerous: *ships becalmed there are at the mercy of any passing robber. But moving back and forth between them can buy time in a chase, or materialize a ship right behind the happiest homebound treasure galleon.*

succeeded in doing with unholy regularity. A couple of times he actually retired from active pirating, thinking he had hoarded wealth enough to support his lavish tastes. But Morgan's avarice was unsatisfied with anything from a civilized existence.

It was greed, pure greed that drove the man. In a trade where equal shares are the rule, Morgan found various ways of keeping the finest portions of booty for himself and contriving things so that his crewmen would get only a few dollars for their perilous work. Time and again, crews threatened mutiny, demanding that their captain more honestly divide the spoils. But Morgan was too successful to lose all favor with his mates. He eventually became very rich, and though it's hard to fathom, King Charles II knighted him!

What kind of captain was this Gaspar Leon? Was he driven by treachery, malice or greed? His smile and fine, gaudy clothes warned of treachery; the elaborate feast spread on deck bespoke greed; his very size and obvious fondness for weaponry hinted malice.

But all he wanted to talk about was food.

Chapter IV

Pirate's Holiday

hy are pirate legends so many? Maybe because pirates love to make legends out of themselves. Often the only thing that stands between a pirate and a knife blade in the back is the fierce manner that is shown to the world.

And it's not just so with the men. Mary Read's mother was a stout English farmwife much plagued by a mother-in-law. The older woman's demands for grandsons drove the poor young wife nearly to distraction. So Mrs. Read rejoiced when her firstborn was a boy. But, as happened too often in those unhappy times, the baby boy died soon after of the grippe.

When her next child was born a girl, she dressed little Mary in blue and knee-trousers, and encouraged a certain affinity in the child for mud and scraped knees. At the age of 13, Mary, in confusion and discomfort at home, ran off and joined the Royal Navy. She used her upbringing to advantage, simulating a man's life. Some years later, Miss Read was crewing on a merchant ship bound for the West Indies when it was taken by pirates. She joined and fought bravely with the band for a while. For the first time she revealed her true gender. Some crewmates howled, but she had proved herself to be capable, above and below decks, and she stayed.

"Fortune's attack sails in a pack."

A MAROONER FLEET setting to battle will find it handy to do so in a line: two ships in a line, or three, protect one other in all four directions. And fortune's captain never sends a single ship into battle unless she means it for a sacrifice, or it's all she has.

Mary Read was as dangerous in love as she was in battle. She took up with one Honest Jake, a good man who was indeed about as honest as a pirate gets. Jake ran into trouble one night in Port Moranto, when a wild-eyed bosun's mate became smitten with Mary.

The two men traded words and drew blades. But before any blood was shed on her account, Mary Read decided things with her own sword, sending the trespassing sailor howling into the night minus one ear.

John Paul Jones was most famous as the father of the American Navy. You might not know him for a ruthless Yankee pirate, but he was that too. John Paul came to the colonies as a runaway from justice, and signed on as a privateer for the Continental Navy. He sailed boldly into British waters, raiding the coasts of England and Scotland. He even sailed up the River Dee in Ireland to loot a castle.

Once after winning a fierce battle with a British frigate, Jones learned that the enemy commander was knighted for his near-gallantry and commented, "Should I have the good fortune to fall in with him again, I'll make him a lord!"

hen you're as despicable as your average pirate, reputation doesn't often rest on people's good opinion. Now, there's one question every Pirateer has to face: "To cheat, or not to cheat?"

Many look down on cheating. Myself, I'm of two minds about it — one when I get away with it, and another when I get caught. But beware: cheating's not for greenhorns. The truly wily Pirateer takes years to learn the craft.

There's others say cheating's a crime, not a craft. Well, my bible is the Pirate's Code of Punishments. Read on:

Drawing a knife on an officer ....*Lose a hand*
Assaulting a shipmate............. *Ducked from the yard-arm*
Stealing..*Head shaved and*
smeared with feathers and oil.
Falling asleep on watch, blaspheming at cards or dice,
rude talk at mess...........................*Flogged or marooned.*

You don't see the word "cheat" anywhere? You may not "blaspheme" at dice, and quite right, but "cheat" has been overlooked.

hile we still have light, let us set out for my home port. We'll be there by dinner tomorrow!" Gaspar Leon called in a raucous shout. "But first, let us begin our salad."

Salad? I'd heard of pirates feeding on many strange things, but never salad.

"Salad! Of course salad!" he bellowed, when I could not conceal my puzzlement. "A meal begins with salad. But you don't know this, and, Monsieur, I am sad for you. We will teach you about salad. Come aboard now!"

With the smoke of their dockside barbecues and bread ovens enveloping our ship, this invitation was sounding better and better to my crew and to me. We all moved toward the lines and planks, preparing to go peacefully over to the other ship.

Gaspar Leon greeted each of us with thunderous back-slapping and a huge grog pot. We soon found it exhilarating to have such a powerful and hospitable new friend. Sitting at the biggest of seven tables set on the main deck, I took a long look at this crew. A happier, more round-cheeked bunch of water-thieves I had never seen.

Before us was a feast of unbelievable richness: fish, all covered in gold leaf, paired game hens with crabs, boar with pike, a whole calf with trout, quails and partridges with more trout, ducks and herons with carp, beef with sturgeon, veal with carp in lemon sauce, beef pies and eel pies, meat aspic with fish aspic, meat galantines with lamprey, then roasted kid, venison, peacocks with cabbage, french beans and pickled octopus.

As we dined, the sun sank toward the horizon and the sky dissolved into banks of red, gold and purple. Twilight, then dusk fell, and torches all over the ship were lit, so that the starry sky seemed a distant mirror of the splendid vessel on which we dined.

That night we followed Leon's ship, the *Terrapin*, to his island fortress on an uncharted scrap of land that offers a generous port in all weather. The buildings were nowhere near as arresting as the opulence of his ship. But I noticed the largest structures were the dining hall and the kitchen, attached in one huge building at the center of the compound.

Our next night with Gaspar Leon was more informative than the first.

After dinner, which he had filled with the most animated talk of warring with the Spanish and wealth that wanted claiming, Gaspar Leon invited me to his den, where he said two other guests would join us.

I ran to follow his enormous strides as he led me to his quarters. Gaspar Leon's lair was like a theater. Mighty carved beams arced high above us, disappearing into the gloom where the lamplight could not reach. On a raised dais stood a mahogany table decked in cloth of scarlet and gold.

Another table was laid with all kinds of sweets, coffees, teas, fruit and ices. Plump velvet chairs lay about the huge table. A silver bowl filled with fragrant dark rum was placed in its center.

Leon rubbed his hands together.

"My friend Ned! Let us talk of things that interest pirates most." He gave me a long, amused stare.

"What have you to tell me?" I asked.

"I wonder more, my friend, what tales you may have to tell me."

"Alas, I have no such tales, good captain, I am only a poor marooner," I said wearily.

Leon laughed. In three great strides he crossed the room to a closet. Throwing open the door, he plucked out — the chair from Skull Island! The mysterious grid, everything was there. I tried to look blandly curious, but Leon just laughed louder.

"Have some rum, Monsieur Ned. You look like you might be dizzy."

I crossed to the table and filled a small tin pot with black liquid. A knock fell on the door.

Don Castillo and Al-Kh'aid stepped up to the captain's table. I knew Al-Kh'aid had released Castillo at Maracaibo. He had his freedom, but apparently at some cost. Adjusting his eye patch and digging the hook he wore in place of a right hand into the table, Castillo took his place at Leon's right. Al-Kh'aid sat at his left. I noticed Don Castillo tried not to meet her gaze.

I could hardly hide my astonishment, but luckily I was given a mask. Leon filled everyone's cup, and urged disposing of the mix as fast as possible. This, it appeared, he meant to continue for some time.

Our talk grew louder. Soon it broke into jagged pieces of song, and whooping. Don Castillo said he would favor us with a *tarantella*.

"Gentlemen, I was a court singer in Madrid before I came to this uncultured place," he said by way of introduction, and Leon practically broke the table with the fury of his laughter.

"He was swimming in the ocean like a rat when we found him and fished him out," he howled. "That's what my watchman told me: '*Mon capitan*, at first I thought I saw only a big rat.'"

The whole company now roared at the memory, but Don Castillo merely gathered in his breath and began singing in a raucous voice.

Now anchors aweigh on a cruise for the pay
And off to Jamaica we run
The sea is my lover, the devil my brother
O-matey-oh ... You'll be a son-of-a-gun!

We'll sharpen our eyes to discover the prize,
Shipping silver and gold by the ton.
And after we board her, we'll give 'em no quarter
O-matey-oh ... You'll be a son-of-a-gun!

With riches aplenty, our friends will be many
To share in fortune we've won.
At taverns we'll tarry and drink 'til we're merry
O-matey-oh ... You'll be a son-of-a-gun!

But soon there's no doubt that our pockets are out,
And we know that our welcome is done.
Then fellow marooner we're back to the schooner
O-matey-oh ... You'll be a son-of-a-gun!

Then it's anchors away on a cruise for the pay —
Sing o-matey-oh ... You'll be a son-of-a-gun!

Don Castillo's song fired my tipsy heart, even as I remembered him standing on the quarterdeck working the lash. I leaped on the table, whirling in time to Castillo's booming voice. They pounded the table below me. Gaspar Leon roared and shook with laughter. Whirling harder, the room took flight around me. Suddenly, it all tipped to one side. I knew I had left my feet, but what would happen next I could only guess.

My answer came: a loud crash and terrific pain in my shoulder. But I heard my comrades gather, shouting, above me. Leon was very excited and kept shouting over and over: "He must do this again! He must do this again!"

In his enthusiasm, he threw an arm around Al-Kh'aid's waist and lifted her high into the air.

"*Mon aimee,*" he shouted, holding her above his head.

Al-K'haid plucked a heavy China pitcher off a high shelf and brought it down with a ringing explosion on Leon's smooth-shaved skull.

Gaspar Leon lurched sideways, and dropped his load.

"Aggghhh, *mon crane*," he groaned.

I watched him fall and my own light flickered out.

or more than an hour I lay sense-less, for when I awoke, my com-panions were huddled near each other at one end of the table. Their words rolled and pitched like stormbound, rudder-less ships.

"This Ned knows exactly where the trea-sure is, I tell you!" It was Al-Kh'aid.

"My lady," Castillo spoke (and I heard Al-Kh'aid snort), "and kind lord Gaspar Leon, may I suggest certain physical ... *trials* ... might assist our subject in talking."

"**W**inds incline to a wise captain's mind."

THE WINDS ON THE SEAS of Pirateer have a magic to them. Those who know their natures, their inclinations and their improbabilities, have a mysterious luck that others can but envy. Think of them as one rolls the dice. One die sends a ship in but four directions. But a pair of those ever-surprising cubes yields its own world of tacks, charges, feints, retreats, formations. Dice can be used together, to move one ship. Used separate-ly, they can move a fleet. The crafty Pirateer captain looks at all the combinations before for-mulating her move. The wind always blows. It is the cap-tain's intention and skill, when fortune's gales blow and the roll of the dice that shapes the day.

"*Non, non,*" answered Gaspar Leon in disgust. I breathed an anxious sigh. "We need his help. Having him in pieces won't help us."

"He has the emerald, and he knows where to find the rest," Al-Kh'aid continued. "As he slept I heard him say over and over the secret route — a cave, a waterfall, 'Emeralds by the hundredweight ... diamonds piled like gravel from a spade, a golden throne with gems inlaid,' until I nearly went mad."

Was Al-Kh'aid trying to betray me? Or was she working some stratagem I didn't make out?

On and on they went in their drunken talk, circling around with fragments and guesses about the treasure. Whenever one of them would come over to me for a look, I made sure to lie very still, even through some rough kicks to the ribs. Each time they went back for another round, and after a while their words became more and more fuzzy, dissolving like mist. First Castillo's head hit the table, then Al-Kh'aid's, and finally the giant dome of Gaspar Leon.

As the Frenchman's head fell, his words began to unravel a puzzle: "*Mon crane* — the skull — *waits for thee.*"

I grabbed a knife from the table and made quick work of the chair's back. I stuffed the precious swatch of leather into my belt and fled into the darkness.

Chapter V

Escapes

wiftly I scrambled onto the dock of Gaspar Leon's fortress. The *Garcia* lay at anchor 70 yards off. There were no small boats along the dock, only a smelly trash barge. I decided to swim. No sooner had I hit the water than I heard shouting on the deck ahead. I swam under the waves in the dark in the direction of the *Garcia*. My men were under orders to return to the ship when the banquet was over, and I could tell by the number on watch that at least some had obeyed.

Now we would slip away — but as soon as I looked out to sea, I saw my plan had already failed. There, silhouetted in the moonlight, cruised the black xebec and the iron-spiked corsair, Don Castillo's ships! Now I knew that treachery had been in Leon's heart from the first. The vessels he said he'd destroyed sailed before me now and blocked the *Garcia's* way. Beyond them, two French frigates reinforced the Spanish blockade.

"Gooseneck is ambition's wreck."

MANY A JOLLY HEIST has come to a sad end in the Gooseneck, that narrow *stretch just before each harbor entrance. It's a patient captain as can hold her treasure ship on the open sea, and not take her first chance at a run home. But defend your harbor lanes well, and choose the wind you sail on.*

By now my crew had seen the ships as well, and they stood looking at each other in dismay. My mind flew. The alarm would sound any moment leaving the *Garcia* and her crew trapped between the *Terrapin* and four other enemy warships.

Running to the rail, I looked toward the castle to see if there were any sign that my escape had been found out. All was quiet.

First I smelled it. Then my eyes fell upon a sight both awful and, now it seemed to me, wonderful to behold. Just beside the dock, only a few yards from where we lay at anchor, the trash barge sat low in the water. It was loaded with a cargo most foul: carcasses and remains of the birds and beasts Leon had had killed for his giant's feast. This mess sat ready to be towed out to sea.

But I had another use for it. First, I ordered all but a few of my crew into the long boats. Within minutes they were rowing with all speed and silence toward a sheltered inlet just down the coast. I and the men who remained now set to the most disgusting work we'd ever performed. In sacks, buckets, nets, we loaded the reeking muck into the *Garcia's* hold. Where thirteen lifetimes worth of treasure once sat, now the stench of death ruled.

We worked fast, and within an hour our grisly task was done. I thanked heaven Leon had forced his party to drink so much grog. No one yet noticed I was gone. Now there was time to set my plan in motion. I had my skeleton crew set sails

"Harbor, port, last resort."

THE TRUE CUTTHROAT can wreak devilish havoc by attacking rivals right in their own harbors. Many an antsy buccaneer sends a single ship out seeking fortune, but leaves the rest idle at home. That's the time for the enterprising captain to slip in where she's not expected, or wanted. There's nothing quite so satisfying as seeing an enemy's harbor cluttered with its own sunken ships.

as if we were headed straight out to sea. Then I sent them to the final waiting boat, and told them to row off a ways and wait for me.

I cut the mooring lines and the *Garcia* started her short final voyage. Straight toward the xebec I sailed her, and watched as the crew of that ship first gaped, then ran to their guns.

When I saw both ships were turning their guns toward me I lashed the tiller fast and leaped over the side. Moments later the barrage began. I didn't have to look; I couldn't look. I knew my *Garcia* was coming to pieces. In the powder flashes timbers, rope, and tattered sails splashed down all around me. Her fresh and grisly cargo scattered far and wide as well. When the sharks arrived, my enemies would think that was the end of the *Garcia* and her crew.

In a nearby cove my mates and I met up with the rest of the crew. From hiding places deep in the jungle the next morning we watched as the *Terrapin* joined her squadron and headed out on another mission of mischief.

I t might be a disappointing thing to discover, but most pirate attacks are bloodless. The mere terror of such savaged-faced and brawny fighters leaping aboard a merchantman with its mild breed of sailor was enough to win most hands. There were times, of course, when a fight was a fight. That's when a few moments' bravery or cowardice can gain or lose a captain's rank, not to mention her ship.

When a treasure ship did turn to fight, it usually meant she had protection nearby. Such a scene greeted L'Ollonais when he encountered a fleet of Spanish galleons near the eastern cape of Maracaibo in the 1720s. The cargo ship carried coconuts from Puerto Rico, and the Frenchman resolved to avail himself of that treat. Bidding his companions, a squadron of French caravels, to wait at the harbor mouth, he advanced alone on three Spanish ships.

L'Ollonais knew the Spaniards would recognize his flag. Many times before, his appearance alone had been be reason enough for surrender. But the Spaniards, well-armed and sup-plied with powder, shot and sailors, were inclined to fight.

L'Ollonais closed with them and began the exchange of broadsides. His method in cases such as these was to stand and fight, always the one to chase. And by this method of con-stant attack, L'Ollonais found the odds fell to him most easily.

The cannon fire lasted three hours. When it grew quiet, two Spanish men-of-war limped to a sheltered spot in the harbor. The coconut ship belonged to the voracious L'Ollonais.

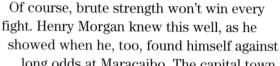

Of course, brute strength won't win every fight. Henry Morgan knew this well, as he showed when he, too, found himself against long odds at Maracaibo. The capital town of that island lay on the banks of a lake which was connected by a narrow channel to the sea. At the opening of the channel stood a fearsome castle that all over sprouted guns and other devilish machinery of war. Four hundred Spanish conquistadors lived in that castle. Morgan vowed to spite the Spaniards by sailing past their stronghold and ravaging their town.

He slipped past a Spanish squadron at dawn with three small frigates, taking the yawning castle sentries by surprise. Morgan moored in the shipping channel that led to the port. He then started to threaten the town with all sorts of terrible fates. His plan, as always, was that her citizens would offer him every last ounce of their treasure.

Holding Maracaibo's capitol with his knife to its throat, Morgan still found himself in a tight spot. He couldn't really attack the town. Soldiers from the castle would overwhelm him once he left the water. Neither could he escape. There would be no sailing past the castle sentries a second time.

He told his crew to seize a medium-sized vessel from the harbor and fit it out as a fire ship. A fire ship! The crew rejoiced, for fire ships are among a pirate's favorite ploys. Procuring a small trader, Morgan's crew filled her up with sulfur and pitch and all kinds of explosive and dangerous things. Next, they rigged her sails and tied them down, trusting just in the moment's wind, for the direction in which they wanted to go.

Now most of the pirates dove off and swam back toward their ships. A small band stayed aboard and ran about looking

---

as though they were running the craft, when really they had as little control over it as a turtle does of the log it rides. They drew near the Spanish squadron, and the Spaniards let them come on. It made these proud sailors laugh to see an upstart who thought himself equal to them.

"They mean to board us!" the cry went up. These sailors beckoned and hallooed as the fire ship approached. Not until the last pirate dove into the sea, did these sailors see the trouble they were in.

By then it was too late. The fire ship, pouring smoke from every hatch and porthole, piled into the lead vessel and cracked open like a brilliant egg. Flames spread over the galleon at once. A slick of fire burned in all directions around the wreck. A second Spanish ship was ignited by the surrounding blaze and retreated in terror. The third Spanish ship beat a quick path out to sea.

Facing disaster, the soldiers' hearts sank. The sun set that night on burning wrecks, half-sunk on the shallow lake bottom. The buccaneer's ships were lit up with torches of celebration.

Still, Morgan's pirates were trapped. The castle and its guns, and the final Spanish man-of-war, stood between them and the open sea. So the Captain set another plan to work. He waited until dusk and then his men started making a show of great activity. They lowered the boats and rowed them to the shore and back in a furious hurry, carrying crates into

the thick brush.

Naturally, the Spanish suspected an attack. And when this ominous activity went on well into the night, with apparently no attempt to hide it from them, the soldiers panicked. At any minute, Morgan's pirates might appear out of the jungle and surround them. At close range, their giant cannon were no use. So they wheeled the great guns around and pointed them toward the jungle, thinking to catch the marauders at a distance and not have to see their ugly faces.

Morgan watched the castle tower with great delight. After a little while, he called back his men and told them to get ready to weigh anchor: they were leaving when the tide turned. His crew looked at him in amazement. But having desperate trust in their captain, the crew did what they were told.

In less than an hour the tide did turn. Very quietly, the three pirate ships weighed anchor, and began to drift. It's a trick of the light that ships drifting on the tide often seem not to be moving at all. By the time they noticed Morgan was moving, the Spanish were in an even more awful state. They knew they could never roll their guns back again in time to train them on the escaping marooners. All they could do was stand and look down on the passing ships, and chew on defeat.

Chapter VI

Grateful Ned

or many years after, I roamed the seas. A map, a slip of hide covered with alien symbols, a treasure manifest, were my constant companions. Castillo and Leon were my constant pursuers. It didn't take long before they found out my ruse. When he returned from his cruise, Leon found one of his small frigates gone, and a farewell note

from me in the form of a looted pantry.

Well they knew the treasures I carried, and the even greater treasure to which I could lead them.

Of ships gained and lost I could tell, treasure won and wasted. But eventually I came to that place where all pirates must. Down to a single leaking pinnace and a surly crew, there came a day even I asked what good was the life of a Pirateer?

It was then that my fortune turned. In the hour just before dawn, while we were lost in a fog bank off Barbados, the *Terrapin* appeared. She trailed an old beat-up sloop behind that ran low in the water. It was bait meant for me, I knew. I meant to take it. We were running dark, and slipped a short distance away unseen.

We formed a party of raiders and I told them to set off in our long boats toward the sloop in an hour. Then I went over the side.

I swam to the sloop, climbed her hull and sprinted to the nearest hatch. One passageway inside was lit and I followed it, guessing what I would find. It ended with a flimsy old door. One shove with my boot and I was inside. A grin spread over my face. There was the empty trunk, still locked.

"One lock be thy key ... " I wedged my fingers underneath the latch. A pull, a twist, then another pull and the prize slid free of the latch. The lock — the key — was in my hands.

Then it was that I heard the small voice that nearly wrecked my schemes.

"Thief! Spy!" A wild-haired little girl stood in the doorway with a sword-belt over her shoulder and a peach-knife in her hand pointed at me. I puzzled over her for a moment. Then in a single crouching leap I hurdled her and set out for a hiding place.

That is where you met me first, reader, crouched among the rotting timbers of that old sloop. But my fortune was not to die there and leave my story to the sea.

One hour passed, then two. Above me Leon's sailors scoured the decks, searching everywhere. But when finally my ragged crew reached the ship, it sounded like a swarm of hornets had descended on the deck. I looked up from my tablet and smiled.

oon reunited with my mates, we tore through the ship like lightning. At first, we met without much trouble. Apparently our small band had fallen out of sight. We reached the sloop's quarter deck before anyone stopped us.

But then it was Gaspar Leon himself flanked by two dozen armed pirates blocking our way. It seemed his whole crew had followed him over from the *Terrapin* to finish us off. He wore a wolfish grin, smeared with blood and some other awful-looking stuff. He held the largest cutlass I'd ever seen, a full seven feet from hilt to barbed tip. He swung it back and forth, meaning to mow us down like a field of wheat. His cronies' courage flooded back now that they stood with their gigantic captain. My crew and I clustered together in a circle, trying to form one fighting knot.

Then something large and white descended on Gaspar Leon's crew. We looked around wildly for some new attack. Up in the high ratlines, three of our companions called out: "To the *Terrapin!* We'll cast off lines, and we're free!"

I looked up just in time to see Grinning Jack leap from the crow's nest and swing himself onto the deck of the majestic French ship.

Jack and his friends had cut away the main-sail halyard, lowering the boom on Leon's hunting party. The ship that had been bait for us was now their durance vile. Wasting no time, we clambered over the writhing figures wrapped in canvas, and hoisted ourselves along the lines to the *Terrapin's* deck railing.

Now the strongest pirate ship on the Caribbean was ours and Leon was left cursing in our wake with a leaky old sloop. Fortune at last had shown me the way back to Skull Island. I said nothing to the crew about our journey's end. But the crew was full of plans for our brand new ship. When pirates come through a scrape together, they have a much stronger tie than owing money or swearing an oath. So my mates and I were undefeatable warriors and lifelong friends, hungry for nothing so much as a treasure hunt.

We arrived at Skull Island just as the sun rose the day before midsummer. Its beaches were as beautiful as I remembered so many years ago.

Since it was early in the day, we set straight off to the cave. I spotted the waterfall and its hovering rainbow while we still had more than an hour's walk to go. But the last few miles went

> **"Tradewinds are fine for the wayward kind."**
>
> *YOU COULD SAY THE TRADEWINDS are an essential law on the seas of Pirateer. Often times a ship's trapped between them day after day. See, the Tradewinds can't be crossed, only followed. It takes some neat sailing to line up a vessel and take advantage of a quick blow to the other side of the ocean. But while the Tradewinds are a fine place for moving, they're of little use as a position to attack from or defend.*

by without effort. I was shaking by the time we reached the waterfall, and by this time my companions sensed something extraordinary was afoot. When I showed them the cave behind the waterfall, whispers flew: "Treasure!"

I led them inside.

We came packing torches and gear, shovels, rope and baskets with help from a large goat, should we want to carry out anything heavy. We unpacked this gear near the cave's entrance, leaving the goat tethered inside the cave mouth with one sentry instructed to sound the alarm should anyone appear.

When we were ready, we progressed down the passageway until we had reached the room where I had first seen the skeleton, the chair, and the chest. I showed my comrades where I had found these things and then invited them to follow me farther inside.

The great symbol of the star glowed in our torch light over the mighty arch. My crew grew quiet. We pushed on, looking up most of the way. On the ceiling above us entwined figures of humans, animals, monsters — strange scripts and symbols hinting at some ancient terror.

I stared at the grid of characters in my hand. Some seemed to be like those on the walls and ceilings, but nowhere was there any clue as to what they meant. My puzzle deepened when we came across the first door: a massive portal, stone-pillared, stone-hinged. Above this squat entrance — while eight feet high, it was probably fifteen feet across — carved into the rock wall, was a grid almost exactly like the one I held. But I could see they weren't identical. My eyes were deceived by an optical illusion I

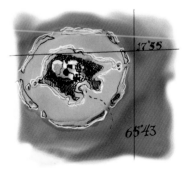

couldn't yet decipher. I stared at the two, one after the other, for a long time. Then we examined the door. It had no handle; the hinges were on top. It appeared to be made of stone from the heart of the mountain.

We quickened our pace in hope of finding the door that matched the grid we held. Several times we were sure we had found its match, only to discover after minutes or hours of hammering, poking and probing, some tiny error in the script that seemed to make all the difference.

We wandered along the tunnel deep into the mountain until the silence and the perfect darkness that enveloped our torch light started to affect us. I halted the company after we had walked for a long time without passing another big door. We gathered close and whispered, although we had seen no sign of life in the cave.

I asked how many wanted to continue, and the fools all said they did. We were just shouldering our packs again when a voice came out of the darkness.

"Take another step and you'll leave this world!"

The voice boomed and echoed in the chamber, repeating the ominous message in a confusion of echoes. I and all my comrades dropped to our knees.

Waves of laughter broke all around us. At first we were even more terrified. But this laughter had no cruelty in it. In fact, it was beginning to seem to me I had heard it before. I stood up and stepped forward. Into the sphere of my light emerged Al-Kh'aid.

Despite the years she seemed not to have aged a day. She stood with one foot upon a tied bundle that lay next to her on the ground. Behind her was a door. Above the door was a grid. I didn't need to check my scrap of leather to be sure.

I was torn between triumph and distrust. Al-Kh'aid's words that night at Gaspar Leon's drinking table came back to me over the waves of time. Now she stood before me, studying me with an amused expression on her face.

"Trying to decide how to get on my blind side?" she chuckled. "While you were lying there, pretending to be asleep, you heard me conspire with Leon, and this." She gave the bundle next to her a kick. It groaned. I recognized the groan.

Castillo let out a pleading whine. "My lady, I am afraid the point of your boot is too sharp for you to kick without denting me severely."

"This one knew," she said. "One of your crewmen deserted and was picked up by the black ship where he told Don Castillo about your treasure song and all the rest. Castillo had filled Gaspar Leon's head full of all kinds of greedy notions so Leon would be sure to throw you in chains.

"I convinced them that I knew about the treasure as well and was only waiting until you led me there so that I could kill you and take it for myself. But I said I had grown tired of waiting for guile to do its work and asked for their help in gaining the prize faster.

"That was the purpose of our meal and drinking bout. We were going to get it from you by drink, and if not that, by less pleasant methods. Knocking yourself unconscious slowed us down considerably. For years I followed these scoundrels as they followed you, thinking you would lead them to the treasure. The Spanish sloop Leon left for you as a trap, hoping you would lead him to his unjust reward. After you disappeared, I stole away as well. I had seen the chair, and it didn't take long to find the cave."

"But how did you come here now?" I asked.

"I watched you capture the *Terrapin* and knew you had gained the last piece of the puzzle. So I finally took my chance, slipped aboard this one's ship" — she gave Castillo another kick — "and took him prisoner so he could do no harm. I shaved his lovely beard," she said, leaning over and pinching Don Castillo's pink cheek, "and used it to brush our footprints from the beach.

"But," she said, turning to the door, " I've seen treasure houses from the Euphrates to the Amazon. Never have I seen one as baffling as this. It can't possibly open. The only irregular spot at all is this slot, here in plain view. That's all it is. A slot. What good is a slot?"

With a wobble in my knees, I approached the slot, fished in my pocket for a moment, and pulled out the lock. I held it against the opening and noticed that they matched in both outline and size. Then I examined the lock — a copper contraption about the dimension and shape of two thumbs placed side by side. It was metal and it had all the features of a lock, but I began to wonder if it was a lock at all.

Putting the object I held in my hand into the slot in the door, I pressed and let go. The metal piece disappeared, and we heard clattering deeper and deeper into the rock. It dwindled to silence, which lasted long enough for the company to start looking around at one another, wondering if I had just thrown our expedition down a hole in the wall.

There followed a tremendous, resonant click, like a giant switch being thrown, echoing up and down the passageway. Deep inside the wall, the sound of falling stones began and intensified until it became a roar. The passage began to shake and drifts of fine dust began to fall from the walls and ceiling. What felt like a subterranean hurricane tore the torches out of our hands.

When we got back our wits, it took many minutes for us to fumble around for the makings of a spark. We scrambled through the rubble, and our stumbling echoed through a vast room.

Finally, with flint, steel and tinder in hand, I lit the head of a torch. The fire blazed up, and and my companions gasped.

It was a sight beyond our imaginings. The walls were plated gold as was the floor, the ceiling covered with thick sheets pounded into the rock. Our torches made constellations blaze off the cavern's every surface and corner. We fainted, we danced, we sang, we came unhinged.

But when that was through, we saw what lay before us. For days, we filled bags with every kind of wealth and trudged down the steep jungle slopes. We stuffed the hold and covered the deck with our haul. There were none but the parrots to gossip on our doings.

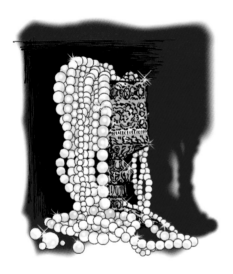

Then came the morning when we readied everything to sail. A breeze had picked up just at sunrise, and our ship, nearly swamped with loot, barely cleared the coral as we pushed out to open water.

But soon we were at sea. I looked back at Skull Island. Its crags and caves were too many and too dangerous to ever be completely explored. And now quite a number of them were stuffed with what we couldn't haul away this time. Thinking of our return, I spotted a glint of rainbow high up on the island peak. The old skull seemed to wink at us as we headed to meet the horizon. In the sea before us, a pod of turtles parted at our approach.

On deck, the crew started to sing.

Pirates dream of one great thing
Of wealth and riches vast.
No mere dream but treasure bring,
Be homeward bound at last.

Fill the sail, set the feast,
Let your heart cheer —
Raise each voice for one great thing:
To be a Pirateer!

The End

The Boot Song

Lyrics by Chris Calder

Music by John Gilmore

G   C7   Fm   Fm#5   Fm

So oft are pir - a - teer - ing for - tunes made,

Gaug7   Cm Ab   1-4   5
                                    G   Gaug Cm

Sail - or file your teeth and grease your blade!   (There's)

There's emeralds by the hundredweight arrayed,
And sparkling sapphires hoarded by the ton,
Pearl fountains and a waterfall of jade,
Sailor file your teeth and grease your blade!

A Mayan throne of gold with gems inlaid,
Bright ingots thick as thumbs and rubied crowns
With diamonds heaped like gravel from a spade,
Sailor file your teeth and grease your blade!

For silver plate we hunger, golden braid,
Let's drink and drown this blasted treasure lust,
With chests of ducatoons that never fade,
Sailor file your teeth and grease your blade!

Speak up hearts, are you buccaneers or slaves?
Are shackles, lock and lash your only wage?
So oft are pirateering fortunes made,
Pirate file your teeth and grease your blade!

One Great Thing

Music and Lyrics by John Gilmore

Pi-rates need but one great thing, To pledge to com-rad - 'ry!
Pi-rates fear but one great thing, Ties that bind too fast!
Pi-rates dream of one great thing, Of wealth and rich - es vast!

Let none hoard nor close - ly cling, But share all e-qual - ly—
Spurned by all who hide in law, We're broth-ers of the mast—
No mere dream but trea - sure bring, Be har - bor bound at last—

Son of a Gun

Lyrics by Scott Peterson

Music by John Gilmore

Chorus sings "You'll be a son of a gun!"

Now an-chors a-weigh on a cruise for the pay, and off to Ja-mai-ca we run— The
With rich-es a-plen-ty, our friends will be man-y to share in the for-tune we've won— At

sea is my lov-er, the dev-il my broth-er, O - mate-y-oh *You'll be a son of a gun!* We'll
tav-erns we'll tar-ry and drink 'til we're mer-ry, O - mate-y-oh *You'll be a son of a gun!* But

sharp-en our eyes to dis - cov-er the prize, ship ping sil - ver and gold by the ton, And
soon there's no doubt that our pock ets are out, and we know that our welcome is done, Then

af - ter we board her, we'll give 'em no quart-er, O - mate-y-oh *You'll be a son of a gun!*
fel-low ma-roon - er, we're back to the schoon-er, O

mate - y - oh *You'll be a son of a gun!* Then it's an - chors a - weigh on a

cruise for the pay— Sing O - mate - y - oh, you'll be a son of a gun!